Ladybird I'm Ready... for Phonics!

Note to parents, carers and teachers

Ladybird I'm Ready for Phonics is a series of phonic reading books that have been carefully written to give gradual, structured practice of the synthetic phonics programme your child is learning at school.

Each book focuses on a set of phonemes (sounds) together with their graphemes (letters). The books also provide practice of common tricky words, such as **the** and **said**, that cannot be sounded out.

The series closely follows the order that your child is taught phonics in school, from initial letter sounds to key phonemes and beyond. It helps to build reading confidence through practice of these phonics building blocks, and reinforces school learning in a fun way.

Ideas for use

- Children learn best when reading is a fun experience. Read the book together and give your child plenty of praise and encouragement.

- Help your child identify and sound out the phonemes (sounds) in any words he is having difficulty reading. Then, blend these sounds together to read the word.

- Talk about the story words and tricky words at the end of each story to reinforce learning.

For more information and advice on synthetic phonics and school book banding, visit **www.ladybird.com/phonics**

Level 4 builds on the sounds learnt in levels 1 to 3 and introduces new sounds and their letter representations:

e u r h b f ff l ll ss

Special features:

repetition of sounds in different words

short sentences with simple language

Ross, Gus and Miss Hill get off the bus.

Miss Hill tells Gus to put his hat on.

It is hot in the sun.

No!

22

23

Story Words
Can you match these words to the pictures below?

Gus
Ross
bus
Miss Hill
hat
sun
log
net

Tricky Words
These tricky words are in the story you have just read. They cannot be phonetically sounded out. Can you memorize them and read them super fast?

the

to

into

I

30

31

summary page to reinforce learning

Written by Monica Hughes
Illustrated by Chris Jevons

Phonics and Book Banding Consultant: Kate Ruttle

A catalogue record for this book is available from the British Library

Published by Ladybird Books Ltd
80 Strand, London, WC2R 0RL
A Penguin Company

001

ISBN: 978-0-72327-540-4
Printed in China

Ladybird I'm Ready... for Phonics!

The Fun Run

Gus, Ross, Mum and Dad
go to the Fun Run.

Gus has a lot of kit.

I am fit!

Ross has no kit and
is fed up.

Miss Hill sets the Fun Run off. Mum and Dad tell Gus to run and run.

Ross is at the back.

Gus runs off but gets hot and has a nap.

Ross gets hot but runs on.

Ross gets back to Miss Hill.
Ross gets a medal.

Gus gets up.

Gus gets back and
gets his medal.

15

Story Words

Can you match these words to the pictures below?

Gus	Miss Hill
Ross	nap
Fun Run	medal

Tricky Words

These tricky words are in the story you have just read. They cannot be phonetically sounded out. Can you memorize them and read them super fast?

to

the

go

I

no

Ladybird I'm Ready... for Phonics!

Gus is Hot!

Miss Hill, Gus and Ross get on the bus.

Gus runs to the back
of the bus.

Ross, Gus and Miss Hill get off the bus.

Miss Hill tells Gus to put his hat on.

Ross and Gus sit on logs.
Ross dips his net into
the bog.

Gus rams his net into the bog.

I am hot.

Ross has a net. It is full of big bugs.

Gus tugs up his net
and it is full of mud.

Back on the bus, Gus is ill.

Story Words

Can you match these words to the pictures below?

Gus

Ross

bus

Miss Hill

hat

sun

log

net

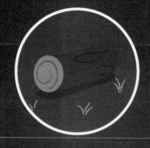

Tricky Words

These tricky words are in the story you have just read. They cannot be phonetically sounded out. Can you memorize them and read them super fast?

the

to

into

I

Collect all
Ladybird I'm Ready... for Phonics!

Captain Comet's Space Party

9780723275374

Not Naps!

9780723275381

Top Dog

9780723275398

Huff! Puff! Run!

9780723275404

Fix it Vets

9780723275411

Dash is Fab!

9780723275428

Say the Sounds

9780723271598

Flashcards

9780723272069